TUG OF WAR

Naomi Howarth

To Jess and Alice, for all the brilliance…
and the occasional tug of war! —*N.H.*

Brimming with creative inspiration, how-to projects, and useful information to enrich your everyday life, Quarto Knows is a favorite destination for those pursuing their interests and passions. Visit our site and dig deeper with our books into your area of interest: Quarto Creates, Quarto Cooks, Quarto Homes, Quarto Lives, Quarto Drives, Quarto Explores, Quarto Gifts, or Quarto Kids.

First published in 2017 by Lincoln Children's Books
First paperback edition published in 2018 by Lincoln Children's Books,
an imprint of The Quarto Group.
The Old Brewery, 6 Blundell Street, London N7 9BH, United Kingdom.
T (0)20 7700 6700 F (0)20 7700 8066 **www.QuartoKnows.com**

A catalogue record for this book is available from the British Library.

ISBN 978-1-84780-851-6

The illustrations were created in watercolour and lithography
Set in Bembo Roman Infant

Published by Rachel Williams
Designed by Andrew Watson and Karissa Santos
Edited by Jenny Broom and Katie Cotton
Production by Jenny Cundill and Kate O'Riordan

Manufactured in Dongguan, China TL042018

9 8 7 6 5 4 3 2 1

TUG
OF
WAR

Naomi Howarth

LINCOLN
Children's Books

One morning, while the sun was high in the sky over the banks of the great African river, Tortoise set off on a walk.

"It's so beautiful and sunny," he said to himself.
"I think it's the perfect day to make a new friend!"

The first animal Tortoise met was Elephant.

"Hello, Elephant!" he said. "Would you like to be my friend?"
"Be *your* friend?" bellowed Elephant. "No, thanks! I am the biggest and best beast in this jungle, and you are nothing more than a small, stupid old tortoise."

Tortoise walked away, feeling sad.

A little while later, Tortoise met Hippo.
"Hello, Hippo!" he said. "Would you like to be my friend?"

"Be *your* friend?" roared Hippo. "Are you joking? I am the toughest, most terrible thing in this jungle, and you are nothing more than a small, wrinkly old tortoise."

This made tortoise feel even worse.

Poor
Tortoise!

Now Bird couldn't help
poking her beak into
jungle business.
"What's wrong, Tortoise?"
she asked.

"No one wants to be my friend because
I'm small, wrinkly and stupid!" sniffed Tortoise.
"Nonsense!" squawked Bird. "Elephant and Hippo
might be big, but you are brainy. I bet you can think
of something to show them that being the
biggest doesn't make them the best."

So Tortoise thought…

and thought…

and thought…

until he came up with
the perfect plan.

"Oi, Elephant!" he said.
"If you think you're the best beast in the jungle, I dare you to hold on to this vine. We'll have a tug of war to prove it!"

"A tug of war with YOU?!" trumpeted Elephant.
"You must be as stupid as you are small."
But Elephant NEVER said no to a dare.

"Hey, Hippo!" Tortoise said.
"If you think you're the toughest thing in the jungle, take hold of this vine. We'll settle it with a tug of war!"

"A tug of war with YOU?!" hooted Hippo.
"You must be as silly as you are wrinkly."
But Hippo ALWAYS said yes to a fight.

Elephant took hold of
the vine and pulled on it
with all his might…

HEEEEeave

And Hippo yanked back as hard as he could…

"Heeeaaaave-hoooo, heeeaaaave-hoooo,

HE E E E E AVE

There was a creaking sound,
and then…

AP!

Elephant and Hippo fell flat on their bottoms!

How could they have been beaten by such a tiny
creature? They thundered off to find Tortoise.

But to their surprise, they bumped smack-bang into each other…

and in that moment they realised what Tortoise had done!

"TORTOISE!" they shouted.
"YOU TRICKED US!"
"You deserved it!" said Tortoise.
"Do you really think that just because you're bigger, you're better?"

Elephant and Hippo looked at each other, drenched
and dripping in sloppy, slimy mud.
"Elephant," said Hippo, "you look ridiculous."
"I doubt I look as silly as you!" said Elephant.

They turned to Tortoise…

… and burst out laughing!
"You might be small, but you're not stupid," trumpeted Elephant.
"And you might be wrinkly, but you are right," hooted Hippo.
"We have been the silly ones!"

"Tortoise," Elephant and Hippo said together, "would you like to be our friend?"

And from that day on, Tortoise, Elephant and Hippo *were* all friends, because they knew that no matter what their size, each of them had their own little bit of brilliance.

Don't miss these other great titles by Naomi Howarth:

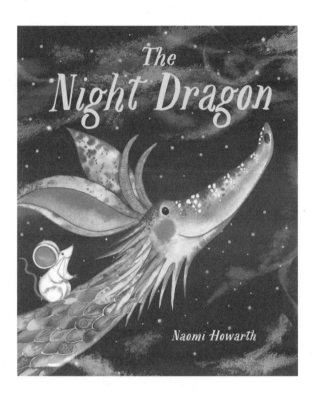

The Crow's Tale

ISBN: 978-1847806154

In the dark depths of winter, snow is falling and the animals are freezing and famished. Brave Crow sets out on a dangerous journey to find the Sun, and beg for warmth. Will Crow succeed, and what will happen to his colourful rainbow feathers?

Inspired by a Lenape Native American myth, this beautiful debut picture book shows how courage and kindness are what really matter.

The Night Dragon

ISBN: 978-1786031037

Maud is picked on by the other night dragons. She doesn't breathe fire, or cast great, grey sooty clouds over the land to bring nightfall. But when the chance comes, will her friend Mouse help her pluck up the courage to fly?